For Lindsey – J.O.
For Elly and Molly, in the land of Oz – L.G.

OXFORD
UNIVERSITY PRESS

Great Clarendon Street, Oxford OX2 6DP
Oxford University Press is a department of the University of Oxford.
It furthers the University's objective of excellence in research, scholarship,
and education by publishing worldwide in

Oxford   New York

Auckland   Cape Town   Dar es Salaam   Hong Kong   Karachi
Kuala Lumpur   Madrid   Melbourne   Mexico City   Nairobi
New Delhi   Shanghai   Taipei   Toronto

With offices in

Argentina   Austria   Brazil   Chile   Czech Republic   France   Greece
Guatemala   Hungary   Italy   Japan   Poland   Portugal   Singapore
South Korea   Switzerland   Thailand   Turkey   Ukraine   Vietnam

Oxford is a registered trade mark of Oxford University Press
in the UK and in certain other countries

British Library Cataloguing in Publication Data
Data available

ISBN 978-0-19-279172-6 (hardback)
ISBN 978-0-19-279173-3 (paperback)
ISBN 978-0-19-279208-2 (paperback with audio CD)

1 3 5 7 9 10 8 6 4 2

Printed in Singapore

THIS book takes its inspiration from the much-loved song 'Here We Go Round the Mulberry Bush': the words can be sung to the same rhythm and there are animal noises and actions, too. It's a book that invites lots of high-energy enjoyment but it's also a book that can be shared with young children to talk about habitats around the world, encouraging them to develop an awareness of the great diversity of wildlife that our planet supports. The book begins with animals you might find in a garden or on a farm. There are also animals from seashore, ocean, desert, rainforest, savannah, arctic and wetland habitats and the book finishes with a group of nocturnal animals in a night-time setting.

Whoosh around the Mulberry Bush

Jan Ormerod

OXFORD
UNIVERSITY PRESS

Lindsey Gardiner

Here we go round the mulberry bush, the mulberry bush, with a mulberry whoosh and a mulberry swoosh.

Here we go round the mulberry bush on a **cold** and **frosty** morning.

This is the way we slime along,
flippety flap and sing a song.

Here we go round the **flower bed** on a sweetly smelling morning.

This is the way we cockle doo, cluck and honk, baa and moo.

Here we go round the chicken coop so early in the morning.

This is the way we **dig** and **dive**, **scuttle** and **Crawl**, nip and **pinch**.

Here we go round the
sandy shore
on a breezy summer morning.

This is the way we flip our fins, swim and swoop, dart and dive.

Here we go round the **deep** blue sea on a **salty bubbly** morning.

This is the way we Yip Yip Yip, Sneak and Slink, woo woo woo.

Here we go round the **tumbleweed** On a **Scorching** desert morning.

This is the way we clack and call,
s-l-i-t-h-e-r and squeeze,
scream and swing.

This is the way we **suck** and **slurp**, **wallow** in mud, **kick** our heels.

Here we go round the waterhole on a **dry** and **dusty** morning.

This is the way we **slap** and **clap,** **slip** and **slide,** splish and splash.

Here we go round the **icicle** on a **sparkling** snowy morning.

This is the way we croaky croak, leap and jump, hop and flop.

Here we go round the mossy log on a misty moisty morning.

This is the way we flit and fly, swoop and soar, big eyes wide.

Here we go round the **starry night** just before the morning.

Let's all do the
mulberry whoosh
mulberry swoosh
and **mulberry** swoosh
around that **bush!**

Let's all do the
mulberry whoosh
every single morning!